MARGRET & H. A. REY'S

Curious George's
First Day of School

Illustrated in the style of H. A. Rey by Anna Grossnickle Hines

Houghton Mifflin Company   Boston

Visit us at www.abdopublishing.com

Reinforced library bound edition published in 2008 by Spotlight, a division of ABDO Publishing Group, 8000 West 78th Street, Edina, Minnesota 55439. This edition was published by agreement with Houghton Mifflin. www.houghtonmifflinbooks.com

Library of Congress Cataloging-in-Publication Data

Margret & H.A. Rey's Curious George / illustrated in the style of H.A. Rey by Vipah Interactive [et al].
    v. cm.
  Contents: Curious George and the dump truck -- Curious George and the firefighters -- Curious George and the hot air balloon -- Curious George feeds the animals -- Curious George goes camping -- Curious George goes to a movie -- Curious George in the snow -- Curious George makes pancakes -- Curious George takes a train -- Curious George visits the library -- Curious George's dream -- Curious George's first day of school.
  ISBN 978-1-59961-410-6 (Curious George and the dump truck) -- ISBN 978-1-59961-411-3 (Curious George and the firefighters) -- ISBN 978-1-59961-412-0 (Curious George and the hot air balloon) -- ISBN 978-1-59961-413-7 (Curious George feeds the animals) -- ISBN 978-1-59961-414-4 (Curious George goes camping) -- ISBN 978-1-59961-415-1 (Curious George goes to a movie) -- ISBN 978-1-59961-416-8 (Curious George in the snow) -- ISBN 978-1-59961-417-5 (Curious George makes pancakes) -- ISBN 978-1-59961-418-2 (Curious George takes a train) -- ISBN 978-1-59961-419-9 (Curious George visits the library) -- ISBN 978-1-59961-420-5 (Curious George's dream) -- ISBN 978-1-59961-421-2 (Curious George's first day of school)
  [1. Monkeys--Fiction.] I. Rey, Margret. II. Rey, H. A. (Hans Augusto), 1898-1977. III. Vipah Interactive. IV. Title: Margret and H.A. Rey's Curious George.
  PZ7.M33582 2008
  [E]--dc22   2007035446

All Spotlight books have reinforced library binding and are manufactured in the United States of America.

This is George.

He was a good little monkey and always very curious.

Today George was so excited, he could barely eat his breakfast.
"You have a big day ahead of you, George," said his friend the man
with the yellow hat.

It *was* a big day for George. It was the first day of school, and he had
been invited to be a special helper.

George and his friend walked together to the schoolyard. Some of the
children were nervous, but George could not wait for the fun to begin.

In the classroom George's friend introduced him to Mr. Apple.
"Thank you for inviting George to school today," the man with the
yellow hat said to the teacher. Then he waved goodbye. "Have a good
day, George. I'll be back to pick you up after school."

The children were excited to have a monkey in class. "George is going to be our special helper," Mr. Apple told them.

And what a helper he was! At story time George held the book.

At math time the children could count on George.

And at recess George made sure
everyone had a ball . . .

and a well-balanced snack.

After lunch Mr. Apple got out paints and brushes. George saw red, yellow, and blue paint. Three colors were not very many. George was curious. Could he help make more colors?

First George mixed red and blue to make . . .

purple.

Next George mixed red and yellow to make . . .

orange.

10

Then George mixed
yellow and blue to make . . .

green.

Finally George mixed all
the colors to make . . .

11

. . . a big mess!

The children thought the mess was funny. But Mr. Apple did not.

"Oh, dear," he said. "We are going to need something to clean this up. Everyone please sit quietly while I look."

13

George did not mean to make such a mess and he certainly did not want to sit quietly. He wanted to help—it was his job, after all. George had an idea.

In the
hallway
George
found
a closet.
In the
closet
he found
a bucket.
In the bucket
he found just
what he needed . . .

15

A mop!

16

George was on his way back to the classroom when he heard somebody yell.

"Stop! Stop! What are you doing with my mop?" The janitor ran after George.

"Stop! Stop! No running in the halls!" The principal ran after the janitor.

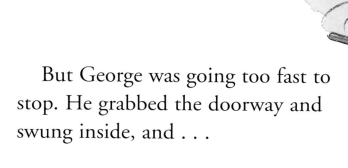

But George was going too fast to stop. He grabbed the doorway and swung inside, and . . .

S
P
L
O
S
H
!

The bucket tipped,
the mop dropped,
and George slid
across the floor.

18

Now the mess was even bigger.

Mr. Apple looked surprised. The principal frowned. The janitor just shook his head.

And George—poor George. He felt terrible. Maybe he was not such a good helper after all.

The children felt terrible too. They did not like to see George looking so sad. They thought he was a great helper. Now they wanted to help him.

So the children all lent a hand (and some feet).

And before anyone knew it, the mess was gone!

"That little monkey sure is helpful," the janitor said.

"It looks like Mr. Apple has a whole class full of helpers," the principal added.

At the end of the day, when George's friend arrived to pick him up, Mr. Apple said, "Thank you for all of your help, George. We hope you will come help us again."

The children cheered. They hoped George would come again too.

George waved goodbye to his new friends. What a great day it had been! He could not wait to come back to school.